ROBIN TO THE RESCUE!

Adapted by TRACEY WEST

Based on the screenplay by
Seth Grahame-Smith and
Chris McKenna & Erik Sommers,
with additional material
by Jared Stern & John Whittington,
based on LEGO Construction Toys.

SCHOLASTIC INC.

Based on the screenplay by Seth Grahame-Smith and Chris McKenna & Eric Sommers,
with additional material by Jared Stern & John Whittington, based on
LEGO Construction Toys.

ISBN 978-1-338-11214-6

10 9 8 7 6 5 4 3 2 1   17 18 19 20 21

Printed in the U.S.A.   132

First printing 2017

Book design by Jessica Meltzer

Hi, I'm Dick Grayson. Not too long ago, I was lonely. I had no family. I dreamed of being part of a family again someday.

Then one night, my dream came true! Let me tell you how it happened.

My story begins in Gotham City Orphanage.
Lots of kids live there. It was hard to feel special.
I knew I had to stand out if I wanted to be adopted,
so I worked on my skills. I wanted to be the best
Dick Grayson I could be.

Two heroes inspired me. First, there was Batman, the ultimate Super Hero. He kept Gotham City safe from crime. Next, there was Bruce Wayne, the ultimate orphan. He had no family, just like me, but he was very successful, lived in a big mansion, and rode around in a limo.

One day, I was outside the orphanage when Batman drove past! I couldn't believe it.

"No way! Look who's here!" I yelled.

The other kids ran toward the Batmobile. They bumped into me and pushed me. I couldn't get close!

"Hey, kids, who wants a shot from the merch gun?" Batman yelled.

Everyone cheered. He shot cool Batman-themed toys into the crowd. But I didn't get anything.

I watched, empty-handed, as my hero drove away.

I didn't let it get me down, though. And that night,
I got lucky!

There was a big party for Police Commissioner
Jim Gordon. He was retiring. The orphan choir was
there to sing for the crowd, and I was part of the
group.

I was singing when I spotted my other
hero—Bruce Wayne!

I ran up to him, and he took a selfie with me.

"Whoa! Thanks, Mr. Wayne," I said.

"Call me Bruce, champ," he told me.

"I'm just so jazzed to meet you, sir," I said. "And I have a question for you. Are you in the market to adopt a child?"

Mr. Wayne wasn't looking at me, and he seemed a little distracted. But he answered, "Yeah." Excellent news!

"One with upgraded features, like cooking, or driftwood art, or street magic?" I asked.

"Sure, that all sounds great," Bruce said as he signed another autograph.

"Do you think you would be interested in adopting me, Mr. Wayne?" I asked.

"A million percent," Mr. Wayne said, looking at the stage where the ceremony was starting.

"This is great!" I said. "Because all I want to do is get adopted so I can stop being . . ."

Mr. Wayne walked away before I could finish my sentence.

". . . alone."

I know that Mr. Wayne walked away from me. But I didn't let it get me down. After all, he *did* say that he would adopt me!

I wasn't going to let my chance to get adopted slip by. So I went outside and looked for Mr. Wayne's butler, Alfred.

Alfred believed me. He let me ride in the Wayne limo. That was swell!

I think Alfred helped me because he knew that deep down, Bruce Wayne missed his family. He wanted Bruce to have a family again.

Alfred drove me to Wayne Manor. It was the fanciest place I had ever seen. And now it was my home!

I ran through the hallways, exploring every room. When I went into the library, something amazing happened.

I touched a bookcase, and the whole thing swung open. There was a fire pole behind it! I slid down the pole. When I landed, I was in an underground headquarters.

I looked around. I saw Batman's vehicles and Batman's crime-fighting tools. That's when it hit me.

I was inside the Batcave!

SECURITY CAM 023
AUTO TRACKING [ON] OFF

FD 35.2987
50mm
10:48:30 AM
TCR 00:21:12:16   PLAY   ZOOM F

"Don't touch that," a voice said, and I turned around. Batman was there!

I couldn't believe it! "Batman lives in Bruce Wayne's basement?!" I asked.

Batman was surprised to see me. "No, Bruce Wayne lives in Batman's attic," he said.

Batman was busy on his computer trying to figure out a problem: how to put the Joker into the Phantom Zone. That's the place that holds the baddest, meanest villains of all time.

"*The Joker can only be put in the Phantom Zone using the Phantom Zone Projector,*" the computer told him. "*The projector is deep inside Superman's Fortress of Solitude, inside a cauldron. Only an object seven centimeters around can fit inside the cauldron.*"

"I can't fit in there. I am way too buff," Batman said. Then he looked at me. "Hey, kid!"

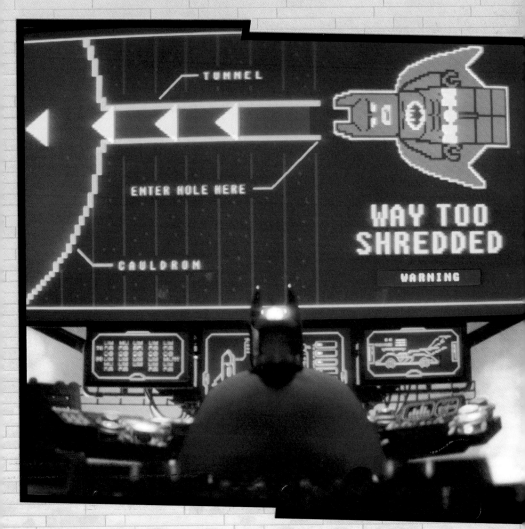

"You're nimble, right?" he asked me.

"Yes," I said.

"And small?" he asked.

"Very!" I said.

"And quiet?" he asked.

"When I desire to be," I whispered.

"Great!" Batman said. "Follow me."
Then Batman walked into a room with all his costumes and gear. "Preparing mission gear," the Batcave computer said. I couldn't believe my eyes!

"Do I get a costume, too?" I asked.

Seeing all the costumes got me excited. I didn't wait for Batman to answer. I started trying them on. The computer named them as I wore them.

The Mariachi. Glam Bat. Clawed Rain.

"No, no, and . . . no," Batman said.

Then I spotted a cool costume called "Reggae Man." It had a red shirt with green sleeves. Red boots. A yellow cape. And green pants. The pants were kind of tight, so I ripped them off. Luckily I was wearing green shorts.

"Now I'm free, now I'm moving. Come on, Batman, let's get grooving!" I rhymed.

We were about to leave when I realized
something. I needed permission from my new dad,
Bruce Wayne, to leave the mansion.

"Well, Bruce and I decided to share custody of
you," Batman said. "So you are mission approved!"

"Woo-hoo!" I cheered. "A month ago I had no dads, then I had one dad, now I have two dads, and one of them is Batman!"

I jumped into the Batmobile. Then it hit me. I was in the Batmobile. Next to Batman. Wearing a costume.

I was a Super Hero sidekick!

"So are you ready to follow Batman and learn a few life lessons along the way?" Batman asked.

"I sure am, Dad Two!" I answered.

Then we sped out of the Batcave, into the night.

We zoomed down the road. Then wings
popped out of the Batmobile and it started to
fly! We soared across the night sky and flew to
Superman's Fortress of Solitude. It looked like a
castle made of ice.

"Superman has zero friends," Batman told me. "So I'll keep him busy while you sneak into that vent and get the projector, got it?"

I nodded. I think Batman was a little bit jealous of Superman, and they didn't always get along very well. I couldn't wait to show Batman all my skills. I crawled through the vent to get to the cauldron that held the projector.

Batman rang the doorbell and Superman answered. He wasn't alone. Through the vent, I could see a big party going on inside. Everyone in the Justice League was there. Batman spotted Wonder Woman, The Flash, Green Lantern, Aquaman, and a lot more.

"Are you really having this party without me?" Batman asked.

The Justice League members all looked away from Batman. It was pretty awkward!

"Um, I guess there must have been a mistake with the email," Superman answered.

I felt bad for my new Batman Dad. I think it hurt his feelings that he wasn't invited, and maybe he realized he should work on his teamwork skills. But we were on a mission. And it was good that the place was so crowded.

I reached a tunnel leading to the Phantom Zone Projector, but it was blocked by lasers. Batman snuck away to help me, and nobody even noticed.

Batman fixed it so the lasers went dead.

"Now do everything I say. Jump!" he instructed.

"Okay!" I said.

Batman and I worked as a team as I flipped, dodged, and somersaulted my way through the razor-sharp claws of the Jaws of Death.

After that, I had to leap through rings of fire without getting burned.

Finally, I reached the cauldron and found the Phantom Zone Projector! I grabbed it and met Batman outside.

"Here you go, Dad!" I said. "How did I do?"

"Watching you . . . out there . . . it made me feel so proud."

"Oh, you're such a great dad," I said. I started to hug him.

"What are you doing?" asked Batman.

"Trying to give you a big old hug," I replied.

Batman seemed a little uncomfortable, but I think that deep down he was happy we were such a good team.

We jumped into the Batwing, and I felt really happy. My days of being lonely were over.

Now I had a family, and I was a Super Hero sidekick, too. And I couldn't wait to have more adventures with Batman!